Inside the Arctic Circle at the top of the world, the sun
never sets during the summer months—even at night.
This is called the **midnight sun**.

SUN DOG

Deborah Kerbel
Illustrated by Suzanne Del Rizzo

pajamapress

First published in Canada and the United States in 2018

Text copyright © 2018 Deborah Kerbel
Illustration copyright © 2018 Suzanne Del Rizzo
This edition copyright © 2018 Pajama Press Inc.
This is a first edition.
10 9 8 7 6 5 4 3 2 1

The publisher gratefully acknowledges the support of the Canada Council for the Arts and the Ontario Arts Council for its publishing program. We acknowledge the financial support of the Government of Canada through the Canada Book Fund (CBF) for our publishing activities.

Library and Archives Canada Cataloguing in Publication

Kerbel, Deborah, author   Sun dog / Deborah Kerbel ; illustrated by Suzanne Del Rizzo. -- First edition.
ISBN 978-1-77278-038-3 (hardcover)
          I. Del Rizzo, Suzanne, illustrator II. Title.
PS8621.E75S86 2018   jC813'.6   C2017-907255-2

Publisher Cataloging-in-Publication Data (U.S.)

Names: Kerbel, Deborah, author. | Del Rizzo, Suzanne, illustrator.
Title: Sun Dog / Deborah Kerbel ; illustrated by Suzanne Del Rizzo.
Description: Toronto, Ontario Canada : Pajama Press, 2018. | Summary: "Young Juno the sled dog pup plays on the Arctic tundra with her boy. Under the midnight sun, Juno is too restless to sleep and goes on a nighttime adventure of her own. When she returns to find a polar bear near the door she left open, Juno must summon all her courage to save her boy and send the bear on its way"— Provided by publisher.
Identifiers: ISBN 978-1-77278-038-3 (hardcover)
Subjects: LCSH: Sled dogs - Juvenile fiction. | Courage—Juvenile fiction. | Adventure stories. | BISAC: JUVENILE FICTION / Animals / Dogs. | JUVENILE FICTION / People and Places / Polar Regions.
Classification: LCC PZ7.K473Su |DDC [E] - dc23

Original art created with polymer clay and acrylic
Cover and book design—Rebecca Bender

Manufactured by Qualibre Inc./Print Plus
Printed in China

Pajama Press Inc.
181 Carlaw Ave. Suite 207 Toronto, Ontario Canada, M4M 2S1

Distributed in Canada by UTP Distribution
5201 Dufferin Street Toronto, Ontario Canada, M3H 5T8

Distributed in the U.S. by Ingram Publisher Services
1 Ingram Blvd. La Vergne, TN 37086, USA

To Jonah and Dahlia, who brought us Freddie.
And to Freddie, who brought us a sun dog
—D.K.

To Molly, Maxwell, Buddy, Reilly, Goldie, Sabby and Sammy, my furry friends both
present and past, and the great adventures we've shared
—S.D.

JUNO and her boy sleep

in a tiny room at the back
of a red house

overlooking a faraway town perched on the edge of an invisible circle at the very top of the world.

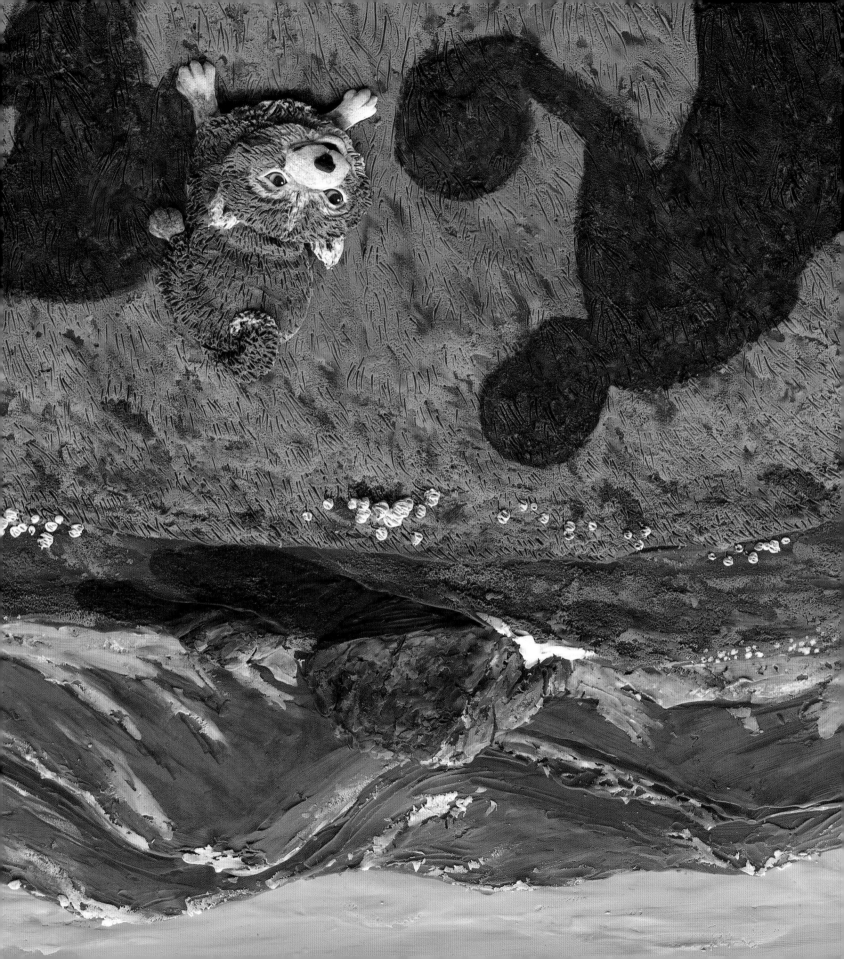

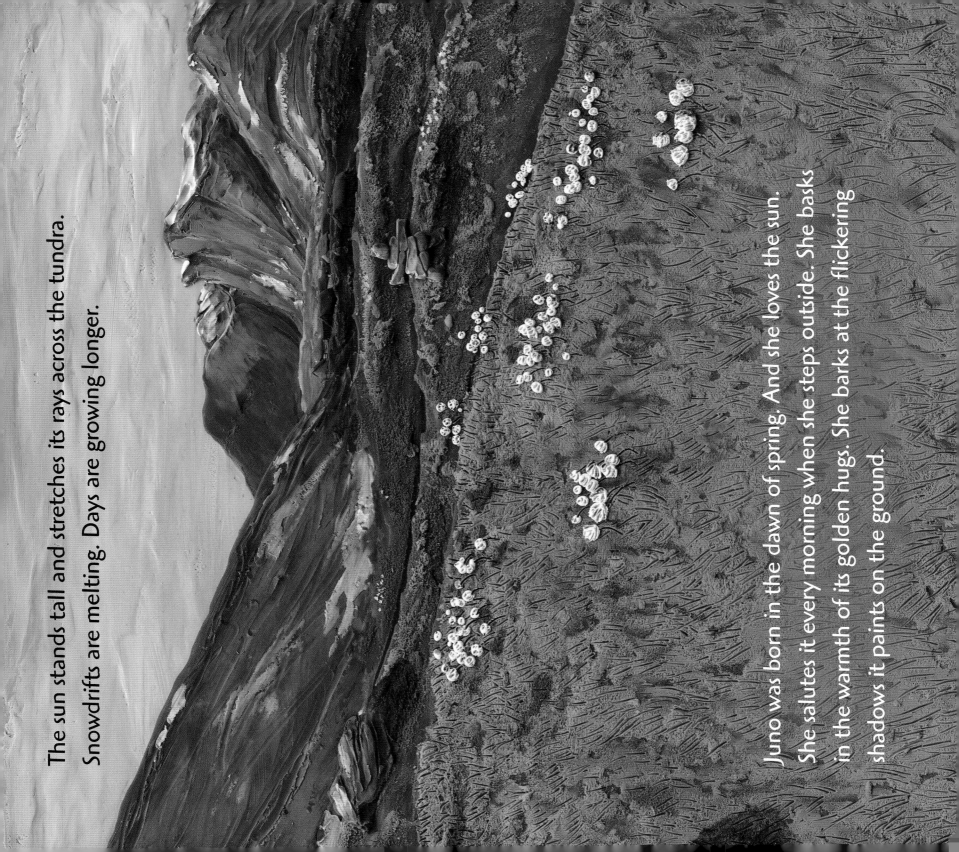

The sun stands tall and stretches its rays across the tundra. Snowdrifts are melting. Days are growing longer.

Juno was born in the dawn of spring. And she loves the sun. She salutes it every morning when she steps outside. She basks in the warmth of its golden hugs. She barks at the flickering shadows it paints on the ground.

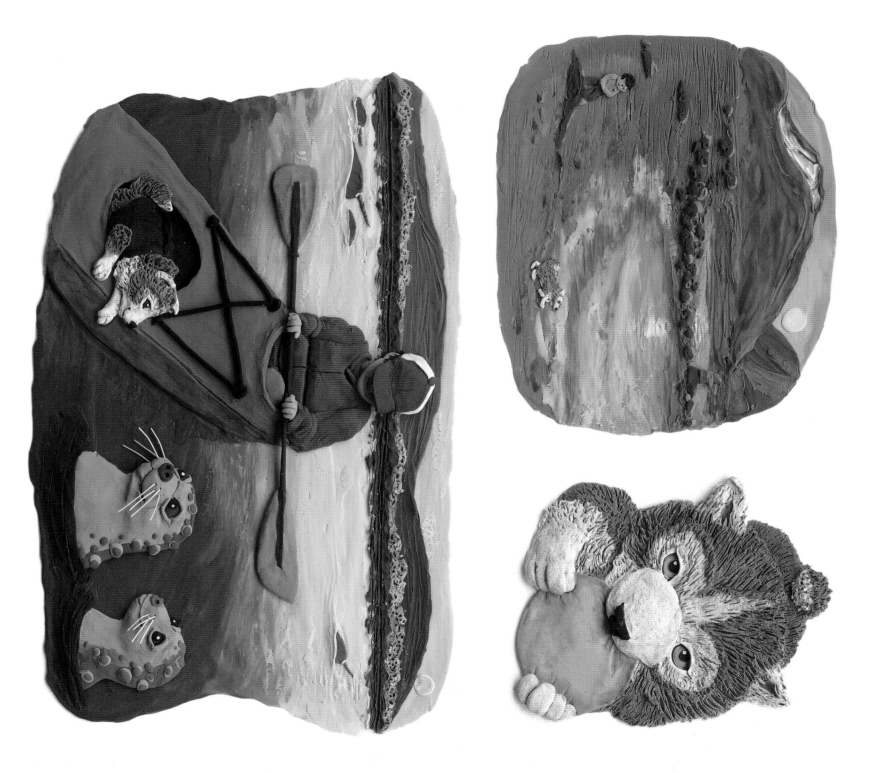

Juno loves her boy. And Juno loves to play!

In between games, she watches the big sled dogs in the neighbor's yard. She wants to be just like them one day.

"You're still too little, Juno,"
says her boy with a laugh.

Juno might be little, but there's a big dog inside her. She knows because it comes out every evening after dinner.

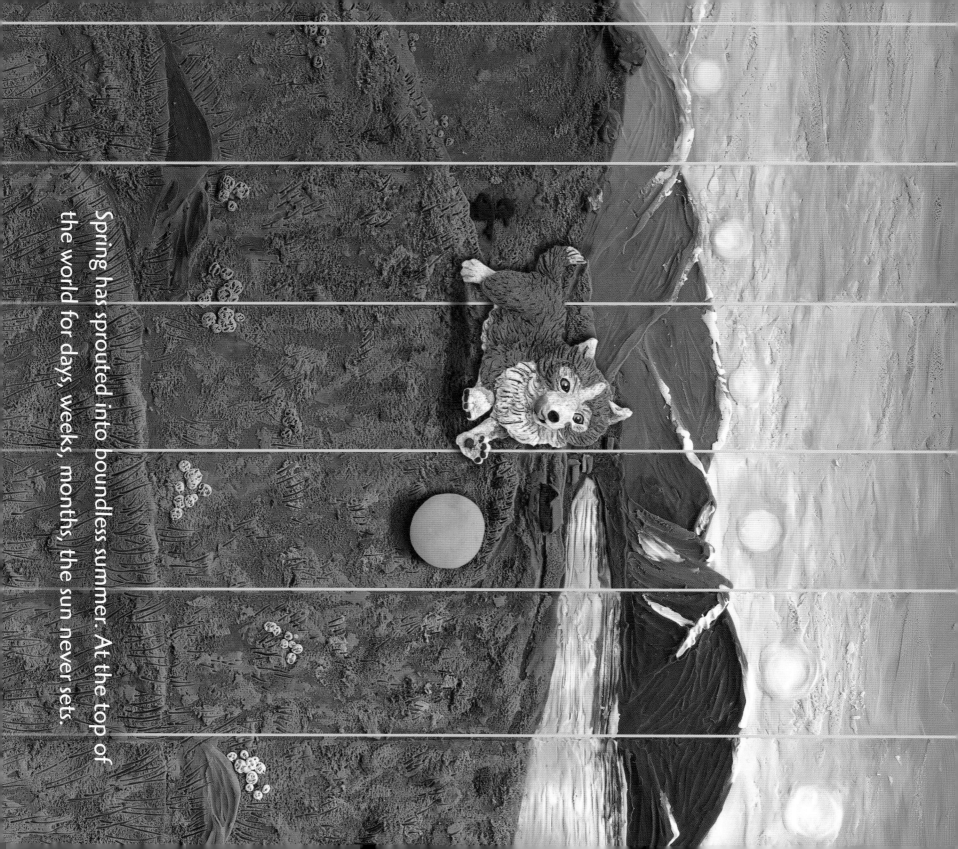

Spring has sprouted into boundless summer. At the top of the world for days, weeks, months, the sun never sets.

Juno whines when her boy says it's time to stop playing.
The sun doesn't have to go to bed now. Why does she?

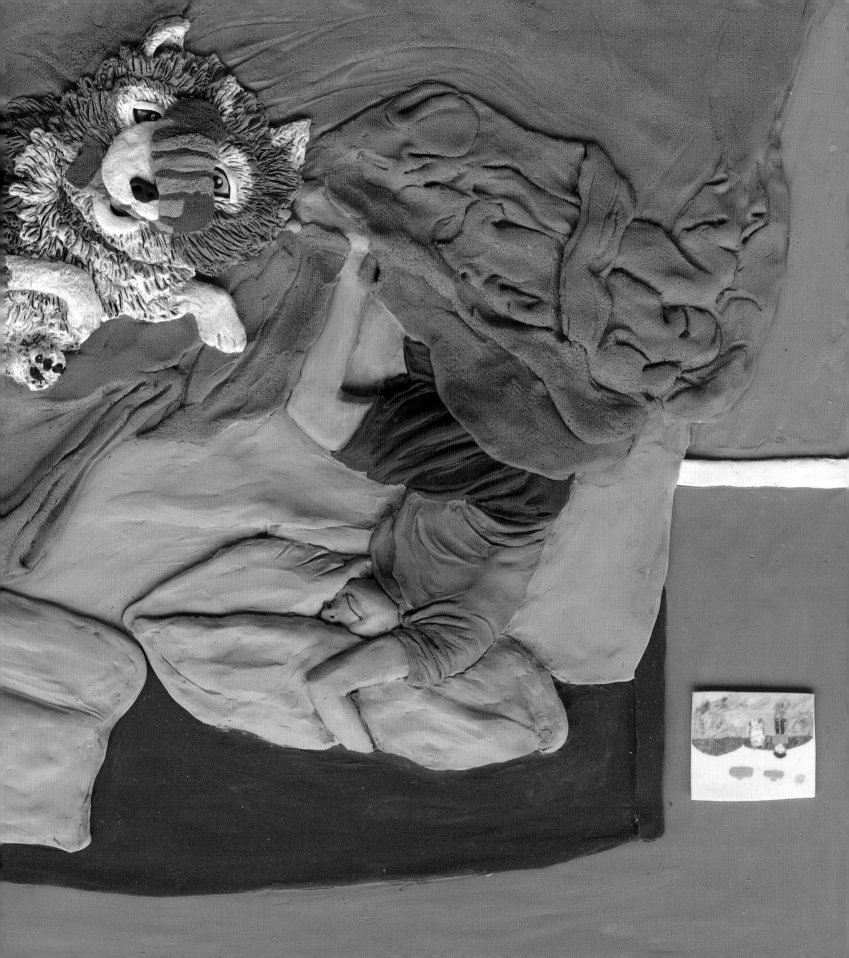

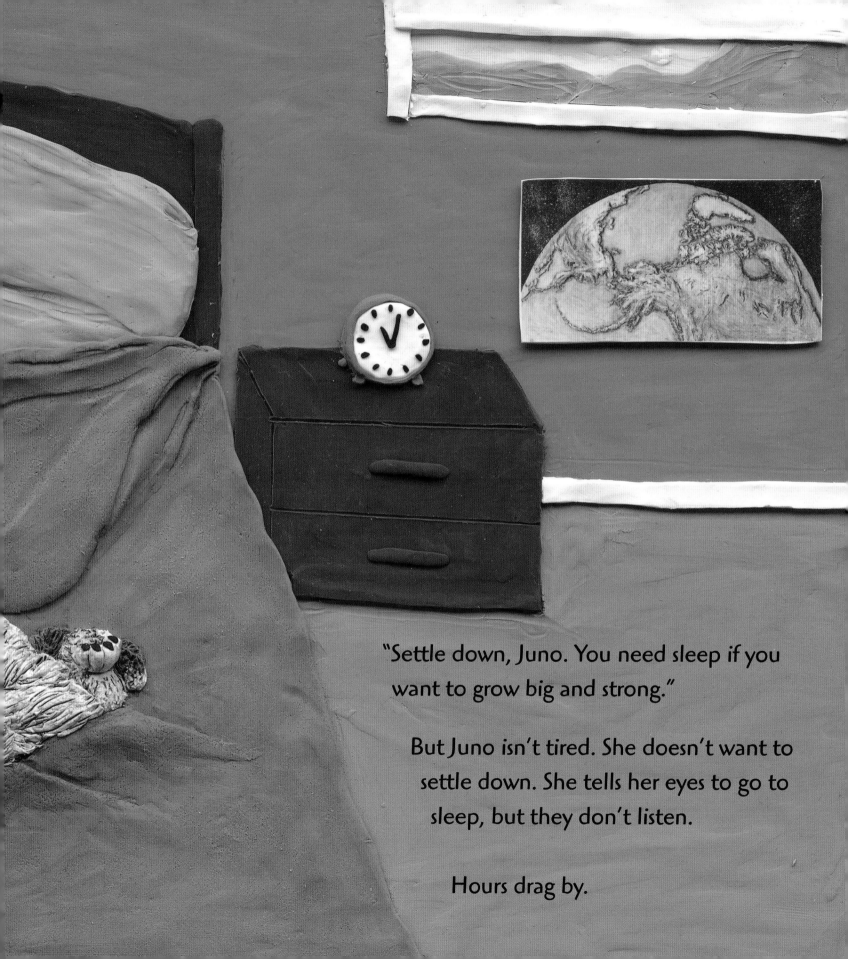

"Settle down, Juno. You need sleep if you
want to grow big and strong."

But Juno isn't tired. She doesn't want to
settle down. She tells her eyes to go to
sleep, but they don't listen.

Hours drag by.

The sun is still up.
So is Juno.

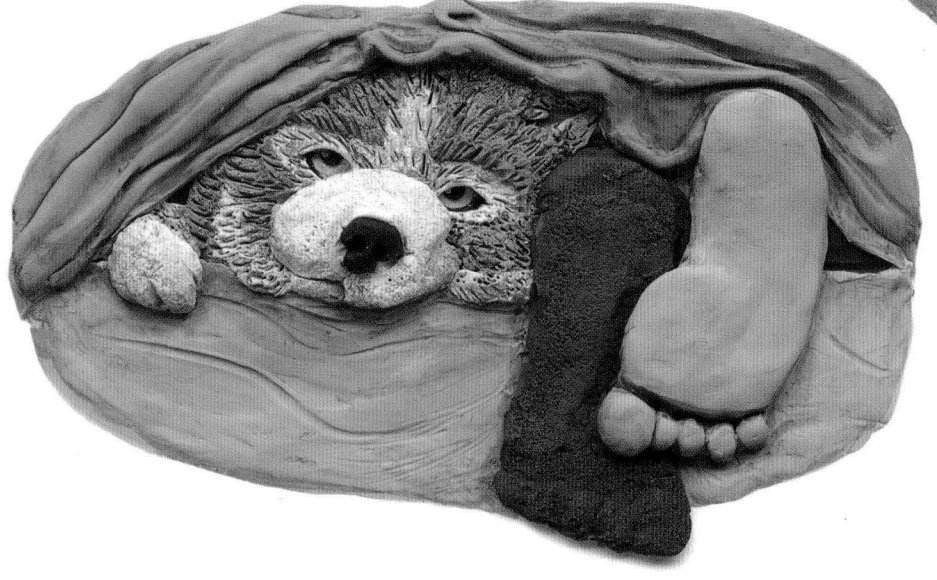

Her puppy legs
are itching to play.

Sneaking out of the tiny room,
she pushes the back door open
with the tip of her nose, and
slinks into the outside.

Juno's tail dances with excitement.

The sun looks like a yellow ball
bouncing low over the mountains.
The sand-colored sky is like a wide-open
beach. The air is as soft as a whisper.

The rabbits are snuggled deep in their burrows.

The seals and narwhals are cozy in their watery beds.

But oh—somebody else is awake! With a WHOOSH and a FLASH,
a pair of ghostly wings swoop down over Juno's head.

This snowy owl isn't looking for someone to play with.
He's looking for his next meal!

Zig-zagging this way and that, Juno ducks and dodges the owl.

She takes a few minutes to catch her breath. It's strange to be outside without her boy. She feels like an iceberg adrift on a giant sea.

She stops short in front of the red house. A polar bear is circling the yard, sniffing for food.

As soon as she knows it's safe, she dashes home as fast as her puppy legs will carry her.

Juno left the back door open.
Her boy is in danger!

Lifting her nose to the sky, Juno barks a sharp warning.

The bear looks around.

His hungry eyes spot the puppy.

His nose twitches.
The bear licks his lips and starts walking. Right toward Juno!

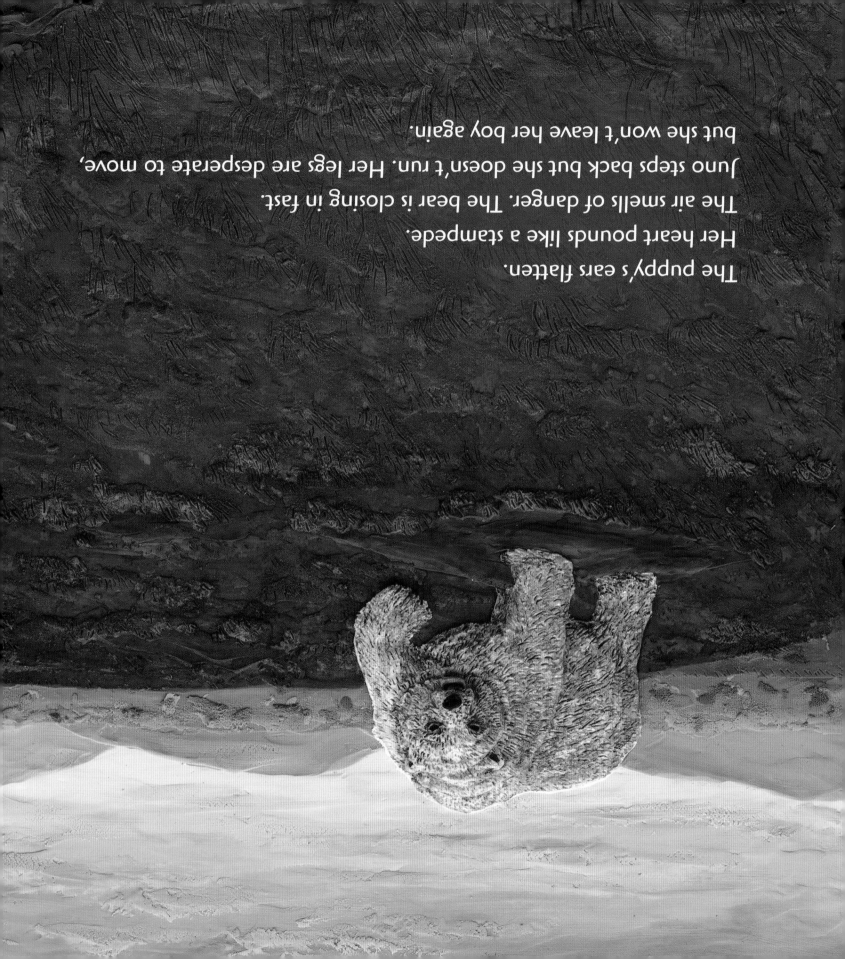

The puppy's ears flatten.
Her heart pounds like a stampede.
The air smells of danger. The bear is closing in fast.
Juno steps back but she doesn't run. Her legs are desperate to move,
but she won't leave her boy again.

She barks a second warning.

A third.
A fourth.
Her bark grows

bigger and **louder** until it echoes across the very top of the world

and wakes the neighboring sled dogs.

They spring from their beds.
An army of fur and fangs rally around Juno.
A storm of barking shatters the midnight sun.

Lights flicker in the window of the red house.

The bear freezes.

With one last glance at Juno, he turns away and lumbers off
toward the shore.

The puppy waits and watches until she knows he's really gone.
One of the sled dogs nudges Juno with his nose.

Nice work, pup.

Juno scurries back inside and nestles
down with her boy.

The sun is on the rise again. And she's
not tired. Not at all.

But she'll close her eyes anyway.
Because it's been a long day.
          And the big dog inside her needs a little bit of rest.

Sometimes when the light is low in the sky, it bounces off crystals of ice high in the atmosphere and causes bright spots to appear on either side of the sun. These spots are called **sun dogs**.

She wanders through town. But nobody else is awake.

Where will she go first?

What will she do now?